SPOOKY POEMS

James Carter is officially the wildest poet and guitarist in any town anywhere. He travels with his guitar, Keith, to schools, libraries and festivals all over the UK and abroad. A long time ago he had hair, very long hair, and he briefly played guitar in an extremely loud and nasty rock band; their single went to Number 3 in the Welsh heavy metal charts. Oh yeah! A while ago, James was staying in an old hotel near Hereford. Some poet called Brian Moses told him it was haunted. Though James likes to think that he doesn't really believe in spooks, he got no sleep whatsoever. Thanks, Brian!

jamescarterpoet.co.uk

Brian Moses spends much of his time presenting his poetry and percussion show in schools, libraries and theatres. His Macmillan poetry books have sold over 1 million copies. He has made many visits to the Channel Islands, where he once lived for a week in spooky Castle Cornet on Guernsey. He has also stayed in haunted hotels. Fortunately, in all these spooky locations, the ghosts must have been tiptoeing around because he slept soundly, untroubled by any manifestations.

Contact Brian via his website:
www.brianmoses.co.uk and check out his blog:
brian-moses.blogspot.com

MACMILLAN
POETRY

SPOOKY POEMS

JAMES CARTER & BRIAN MOSES

Illustrated by Chris Garbutt

MACMILLAN CHILDREN'S BOOKS

First published 2015 by Macmillan Children's Books
an imprint of Pan Macmillan
20 New Wharf Road, London N1 9RR
Associated companies throughout the world
www.panmacmillan.com

ISBN 978-1-4472-7258-8

3 5 7 9 8 6 4 2

A CIP catalogue record for this book is available from
the British Library.

Printed and bound by CPI Group (UK) Ltd, Croydon CR0 4YY

*For the spooktacular Mark Hawkins, a fabulous
fiend and a magician of a musician – JC*

*For Anne, my wife and my creative adviser, who
has the uncanny knack of knowing which of my
lines are duff ones, sometimes even before
I've written them. Spooky, eh? – BM*

CONTENTS

SCARIES AND SKELLINGTONS

BONES AND GHOULS

WIZARDS AND WITCHES

AND WILY WOLVES

PLEASE HOLLER PLEASE HOWL

PLEASE MAKE A GREAT DIN –

FOR SPOOKY POEMS

WILL NOW BEGIN . . .

James Carter

DON'T READ THIS BOOK

This book may well disturb you,
it will creep into your dreams,
for nothing you read in this book
is ever quite the way it seems.

This book may well reveal
unpleasant things about yourself.
If I were you I think I'd leave it
up there on the shelf.

It's a wild and upsetting read
from first page to the last,
a wrong-side-of-the-road trip
as strange ideas slip past.

You'd be far better off not knowing
about the horrors hidden within.
It's an open tomb, graveyard gloom,
it's sorrow and it's sin.

Your parents will be worried
if they see you sneaking a look.
Your teacher will advise you to read
any other kind of book.

So just leave it, don't be tempted,
don't give it a second look.
You're far too nice a person
to read such an alarming book.

Brian Moses

A GOOD SCARY POEM NEEDS . . .

A haunted house,

    a pattering mouse.

A spooky feeling,

    a spider-webbed ceiling.

A squeaking door,

    a creaking floor.

A swooping bat,

    the eyes of a cat.

A dreadful dream,

    a distant scream.

A ghost that goes 'BOO'

    and **You!**

Brian Moses

WHAT TO SAY IF YOU MEET A GHOST . . .

```
              Aaa
            aaaaaaa
            aaaaaaa
!!!          aaaaaa              !!!
 !!          aaaaa               !!
   !!         aaa              !!
    !!      aaaaaaa        !!
         aaaaaaaaaaaaaa
        aaaaaaaaaaaaaaaaa
       aaaaaaaaaaaaaaaaaaa
      aaaaaaaaaaaaaaaaaaaaa
       aaaaaaaaaaaaaaaaaaa
        aaaaaaaaaaaaaaaaa
         aaaaaaaaaaaaaa
          aaaaaaaaaa
          aaaaaaa
            hhhh
            hhh
            hhh
            hh
            hh
            h
            !
            !
            !
```

James Carter

THE FEAR

I am the footsteps that crackle on gravel
and the sudden chill that's hard to explain.
I am the figure seen flitting through doorways
and the noisy rattle of a loose windowpane.

I am the scream that wakes you at night
with the thought, was it real or a dream?
I am the quickening thud of your heart
and the feeling things aren't what they seem.

I am the slam of a door blown shut
when there isn't even a breeze
and the total and absolute certainty
that you just heard someone sneeze.

I am the midnight visitor,
the knock when there's no one there.
I am the ceiling creaking
and the soft footfall on your stair.

I am the shadows that dance on your wall
and the phantoms that float through your head.
And I am the fear that you feel each night
as you wriggle down deep in your bed.

Brian Moses

GHOSTLY BUSINESS

Have you ever seen a ghost?

A what?

A ghost!

Pardon?

A grey ghost?

Sorry?

A gruesome grey ghost?

Errr ... ?

A horribly huge, gruesome grey ghost?

Umm ... ?

An utterly ugly, horribly huge, gruesome grey ghost?

Why?

There's one behind yoooooooooooooou!

James Carter

GHOSTS OF THE LONDON UNDERGROUND

In the subway tunnels
    dying to be found,
on the Circle Line
    going round and round,
in the wail of the wind,
    a peculiar sound,
these ghosts
    of the London Underground.

Down, deep down, down deep underground
these ghosts of the London Underground.

And maybe you'll find
    you can see right through
the passenger sitting
    opposite you,
or a skull appears
    from beneath a hood
and you really wish
    you were made of wood,
that you didn't see
    what you think you did
and all these horrors
    were still well hid.

Down, deep down, down deep underground
with ghosts of the London Underground.

No ticket needed,
    you travel free
in the freakiest, scariest
    company.
Stand clear of the doors,
    we're about to depart,
so block up your ears
    and hope that your heart
is strong enough
    to survive the ride,
we're taking a trip
    to the other side.

Down, deep down, down deep underground
with ghosts of the London Underground.

And the tunnels echo
    with demonic screams
that chill your blood
    and drill into your dreams.
And you can imagine
    only too well
how these tunnels might lead you
    STRAIGHT INTO HELL . . .

Down, deep down, down deep underground
Down, deep down, down deep underground
Down, deep down, down deep underground
these ghosts of the London Underground.

these ghosts . . .

these ghosts . . .

these ghosts . . .

Brian Moses

LITTLE SPOOK

Once there was a little spook
as pale as the moon
and once upon a Halloween
he drifted from his room

He came across a little town
as pretty as a book
he crossed the bridge, flew down the street
and went to take a look

He saw the celebrations
the spooky-goings-on
the jack-o'-lanterns, trick or treats
the children having fun

He loved it all and so much so
he thought he'd do his stuff:
he quivered, shivered, hollered, howled –
the children hurried off!

And now upon a Halloween
beneath a yellow moon
that little spook, he stops at home
alone in his room

James Carter

GHOST WALK
(EDINBURGH: THE CITY BENEATH THE CITY)

For my daughters, who both took the walk with me

This is a place where history
and the supernatural meet,
a chilling place, a haunted place,
underneath our feet.

And we're about to go down there,
into the city of gloom,
to leave behind electric light
and the safety of this room.

Your hand in mine as we follow the guide
who's leading our ghostly walk.
Already we hear nervous laughter
and ripples of anxious talk.

The guide says, 'In this place you may
feel tugging at your coat.'
'Tell me straight away,' he says,
'if something fingers your throat.'

And even though it's warm outside,
down here there's a temperature fall.
'It's a sign,' our guide informs us,
'that the spirits are ready to call.'

And we really want to be here
and, then again, maybe we don't.
Half hoping that something will appear,
half hoping something won't.

Brian Moses

GHOST SHIPS

To solve the secrets of the past
maybe we should ask the stars:
for they're the watchers of the skies
with their ever gazy eyes

To them my question would be this:
what happened to the pirate ships?
Are they somewhere, way out there,
where sea meets sky, and water, air?

Pirates left their lives of crime
but do their ships still drift through time?
And do the timbers creak and groan
as they heave through storms alone?

And what the sails, the flags of bones
cut to shreds and tempest blown?
Come stars, reveal – please do tell all:
do these ghost ships tumble, fall

off the edge of ocean green
through the sky to space serene
and while they glide through endless night –
stars, d'you guide them with your light?

James Carter

DUNOTTER CASTLE
(JUST SOUTH OF ABERDEEN)

This fortress that's built on a rock
is the spookiest of places,
where the Scots could retreat when attacked
and laugh in their enemies' faces.
It's empty now and quite forlorn
but it's still the castle to see –
roofless buildings, empty rooms
and a whiff of tragedy.

The rushing of winds in the ruins
have hollowed out its heart,
I imagine the rumble on flagstones
of a time-slipped horse and cart.
The pigeons in the tower
are spooked by my being here,
they take off and halo the castle,
then swiftly disappear.

In the visitors' book someone wrote:
'It's a miracle, it really is brill,
it sent a chill through my blood,
today has been such a thrill.'
Someone else wrote, 'It's fabulous,
this castle is really the most,
taught us a lot about history,
but pity we missed the ghost!'

And as I left, with the day turned grey
and the great door locked for the night,
I imagined not one ghost, but hundreds,
looking down from the castle heights.
An army of phantom warriors
ready once more to defend
their country from hostile invaders
in a fight to the bitter end.

Brian Moses

HOLIDAYS ON THE GHOST COAST

Why don't you holiday on the ghost coast,
the coast that really is the most
for stressed-out spirits and wilting wailers,
for gloomy ghouls and long-drowned sailors.

From your haunting you could be swiftly
    released
to lie on the beach with a beauty (deceased)
or hover and float above the waves
while sea sprites invite you to visit their caves.

You can meet spooky ladies shrouded in grey,
talk about what you can do all day
with nothing to keep you awake at night,
no place to go to give someone a fright.

You're at rest for the first time in hundreds of
    years,
take it easy, relax, discuss with your peers
how haunting was fun when first you were dead,
how you'd frighten people by removing your
    head.

If you want to, all day you can sit in the shade,
keep yourself to yourself and, when others pass,
    fade
to nothing or no one, be invisible too
if other ghosts call and ask after you.

And when you return, as you certainly will,
to your castle, your churchyard, your house on
    the hill,
you'll feel so much better, prepared once more
to be even ghostlier than you were before.

Brian Moses

NIGHT TRAIN TO TRANSYLVANIA

On the night train to Transylvania
you can
check out groovy graveyards you may have missed
on previous trips.
You can talk to estate agents about buying
your very own mausoleum,
where you'll sleep soundly by day
and then easily escape from at night.
Discuss with other like-minded creatures
the best ways to frighten victims,
how to trick them into baring their necks
and where to bite for the deepest drink.
Discover the comfiest coffins
in which to lie for all eternity.
Be warned in advance of the tricks and
    paraphernalia
of the vampire hunter, of the ways to combat garlic
and avoid a sharpened stake.
You'll meet and mingle with many denizens
of the darkest night, with ghouls and gremlins,
werewolves and warlocks,
so be warned,
that little old lady might be Grand High Witch,
that buffet-car attendant could easily
be Count Dracula's descendent
and even that hairy porter could be Voldemort
(just don't speak his name),
on the night train to Transylvania.

Brian Moses

THE GHOUL SCHOOL

Through the still of the night
you hear it sound,
the ringing of the ghoul-school bell.
Then you leave your house
and creep like a mouse
as if you were held in a spell.

Till the ghoul-school bus
slides to a stop
and you find yourself climbing inside.
Then you hold on tight
as you race through the night
on a wild and spooky ride.

As midnight chimes
the bus arrives
and you enter the ghoul-school gate.
Then with cackles and shouts
the bus empties out
and leaves you there to your fate.

And the ghoul-school secretary
floats in front
as she leads you right through a wall.
You can't be awake,
there must be a mistake,
it's assembly in the ghoul-school hall.

Then your teacher
rattles out your name
with teeth that chitter-chatter.
And she shows you your seat
as her feet click the beat
in a sinister clitter-clatter.

The Head's lost his head
or so it seems,
it's floating about in the air.
It drifts all around
in silence, no sound,
as his body sits down in a chair.

Then you're running away,
with one thought in your head,
escape, it's your only intention.
But you're being held back
by a ghostly pack
who mutter that you're in detention.

And you open a book
that's slipped on to your desk
but the pages begin to burn.
As the flames reach out
you hear something shout:
In this school you'll never learn.

Then the ghoul-school bus
picks you up at the gate
and races you back to your door.
A voice from the bus
screams, '*You're now one of us
and tomorrow you'll come back for more.*'

Brian Moses

MISS GWENDOLEN GRUEL'S PREPOSTEROUSLY PROPER PREPARATORY SCHOOL FOR GHOULS!

Oh, by golly, by golly, by gosh!
Miss Gwendolen Gruel's is *painfully* posh.
And *awfully* prim and *fearfully* fine.
The fees are so *horrifically* high.

The ghouls all curtsy in a line.
They never wail. They're so refined.
Each night they chant (politely too) –
'How-do-you-dooo?' then *'Toodle-oooo!'*

*Miss Gwendolen Gruel's Preposterously Proper
Preparatory School for Ghouls!*

But only the best of beastly ghouls
will make the grade in this great school.
Tiffany, Tabatha, Flavia, Flo
work *dreadfully* hard. *Horrendously* so.

You see, the work of a ghoul is hell –
though cruel Miss Gruel prepares them well
for future lives of doom and gloom –
of haunting tombs and hotel rooms.

Miss Gwendolen Gruel's Preposterously Proper
Preparatory School for Ghouls!

She shows them how to walk through walls –
with shoulders back while standing tall.
But most of all, the way to scare –
by holding heads while climbing stairs.

These ghouls are cool. Know what they'll do?
They'll shake your hand. Be kind to you.
So don't be shocked or spooked, be wise:
those *ghastly* ghouls
are *f r i g h t f u l l y* nice!

James Carter

BRITAIN'S GOT TALONS PRESENTS . . .
HOW SPOOKY IS YOUR TEACHER?

Think very carefully now . . .

COULD SHE BE A *VAMPIRE*? Have you
ever seen her hanging upside down from the
classroom ceiling or snacking on uncooked mice
from her lunch box?

COULD SHE BE A *WEREWOLF*? Check if her
arms, legs and face get hairier after dark. And
does she howwwwwl when in a grump?

COULD SHE BE A *GHOST*? Easy to spot: does
she walk through walls when she's in a hurry?

COULD SHE BE A *ZOMBIE*? Probably
not, but does she randomly pop out of the
ground, staggering from side to side going
'Urgggggghhh!'?

COULD SHE BE A *FRANKENSTEIN-TYPE
MONSTER*? Extremely unlikely this one – but
do her fingers, toes and ears sometimes fall off
during PE?

COULD SHE BE AN *OFSTED INSPECTOR IN
DISGUISE*? Sorry, only kidding, she can't be
THAT gruesome!

If you've answered YES to even ONE of the above,
move class, move school, move to Antarctica and
just keep moving cos she's like TOTALLY got . . .

THE SPOOK FACTOR!

James Carter

EVER WONDERED WHAT'S IN YOUR . . . TEACHER'S CUPBOARD?

Well, open the door,
creak it wide.
Be brave, go on,
just peak inside.

A cobweb catches
in your hair.
The stench is more
than you can bear.

On the ceiling?
Rows of bats.
At your feet?
A squeal of rats.

See jars of blood
with human bits,
the pickled limbs
of naughty kids.

An open coffin,
padded too.
Nice 'n' cosy . . .
room for two.

So peeps, beware,
be oh-so-scared.
Children don't
return from there . . .

James Carter

MONSTERS V MONSTERS

Moments after midnight
Out of bedroom cupboards such
Nightly visitors burst, stomping around your room,
Stealing the very breath from your lips,
Taking your favourite blankie,
Even gatecrashing your dreams,
Raging and rampaging after you like dark storms.
Still – we know that's not true, don't we?
Maybe these beasties exist after all:
Only not as we think that they might.
No, they would be invisible, more
Silent than stars, more
Tricky than shadows, they'd lurk,
Eating away in cold corners of our minds,
Ridiculing us, informing us that we are useless.
So. What to do? Ignore them. They'd *hate* that.

James Carter

SLEEP

Sleep is a city
of towers and walls
a forest of whispers and
charming young wolves

Sleep is a castle
of shadows and mist
a century burst by
a spell-breaking kiss

Sleep is a dreamer
as well as a guide
through gardens and mazes
and maps of your mind

Sleep is a potion
not poison, but kind
to help you escape
leave night-time behind

Sleep is a cloud
adrift on the land
a trickle like silver
that slips through your hand

Sleep is a nest
and a rest deep and lush
a heartful of wonder
a headful of hush

James Carter

BAD DREAM?

Are you trapped inside
a sunken ship?

Have you seen
a faceless face?

Are you on the run
from a gaggle of ghosts?

Did you watch
your soul escape?

Are you lost in a mist?
Are you stuck in a lift?

Did you float
on a blood-red lake?

Let's hope
it's a dream

for if it's not,
you must be

awake . . .

James Carter

ALONE AT NIGHT

Left alone at night,
the landing light on,
still knowing there are two dark rooms
that something could creep from.

Snuffles and snorts from the garden below,
screams from the TV downstairs,
imaginary eyes in the gloom,
unexplained rattles and creaks.

Something in the loft
sliding open the hatch,
tendrils dangling down and
reaching out to strangle me.

Something beneath my bed
suddenly wakeful,
hearing its breathing,
the scratching of claws.

Something in the wardrobe,
sharpening its axe,
doors slightly open,
the axe about to fall.

Something climbing on to my bed,
feeling its pressure against my feet,
If there's ever a moment to scream
it's now . . .

And I do . . .

AAAAARRRRRGGGGGHHHHH!

Brian Moses

ABOVE THE PIT

From my childhood room I stared at the street,
lit by the glow of a werewolf moon,
past the lorry yard to the mission hall,
where tall gates were padlocked tight.
Beyond, I knew, were graves in the grass,
a garden of rest that no one tended,
fastened to keep the curious out
or sinister somethings within.

Now rough feet tramp over ground
no longer sacred. The graves are gone,
shuffled and stacked like cards
then cleared away. They levelled the land,
then sank foundations firm enough
to stand new houses.

And I wondered how deep they'd dug,
remembered what I'd read
of men who moled the London Tube
and how their spades uncovered bones,
the final homes of those who went
plague naked to the burial place.

I was certain no good would come
from building houses over a graveyard.
Already the ground was spread with cracks,
driest summer for twenty years,
but it seemed to me like a scene being set
where everyone's watching TV and then . . .

The carpet buckles, bursts apart,
an arm reaches up
from the pit . . .

Brian Moses

WILDERNESS HILL

Children never go there
and traffic never slows
on Wilderness Hill.

Winds blow cold there
and stories are told
about Wilderness Hill.

Birds never call there,
avoided by all
is Wilderness Hill.

Flowers never grow there
but everyone knows
about Wilderness Hill.

Don't You?

Brian Moses

THE GATHERING

What strange and secret gathering
has met beneath this tree
on Humpback Hill
by crimson moon
for midnight revelry?

What souls sat here, what hoofs, what claws,
what feral friends came dine
nature plotting
dark revenge
such mischief on mankind?

What ghastly magic did they spin
round fire of spark and flare
those gatherers
as real as flesh
that rose then turned to air?

James Carter

THE TRACKS AND THE TOMBSTONES

Our classroom lay between
the tracks and the tombstones.

On one side
electric trains
ploughed the line to London.
On the other
a graveyard
beckoned uninvitingly.

One offered hope,
climb on board, get away.
The other mocked,
don't bother, don't try.
This is your ultimate destination,
graveyard, not railway station.

One side was noisy.
Messages hummed in the rails:
a clatter on the tracks,
a zing in the lines,
a hell of an interruption.

The other was quiet,
not quiet quiet,
just lifeless.

And we could be lifeless too.
Our teacher would joke:
'There's more life out there
in that boneyard
than there is in you lot today!'

But when we wanted,
we could be dead quick:
we'd play about
when the teacher was out,
knowing that no one
was keeping an eye . . .

Trains move too fast,
the dead don't tell tales.

Our classroom lay between
the tracks and the tombstones.
Our classroom lay between
the quick and the dead.

Brian Moses

WHO HAUNTS THIS HOUSE?

Who haunts this house?

I do . . .

I hover in the hall, hoping to hear
the house's secrets.

I settle on the staircase
like a shiver of shame, with a story to tell
of a ne'er do well.

I float by the fireplace
giving shape to the smoke
that escapes from the chimney.

I hide behind the wardrobe,
whispering warnings of storms to come.

I fire a rat-a-tat-tat of words
with a mouth that screeches,
sniggers and snarls.

*And who will stay for just one night
with one who must stay
an eternity?*

Brian Moses

ME AND THE GHOSTS

Me and the ghosts were walking in the woods,
with the dead leaves and the fallen trees,
while they whispered secrets
and told me stories
of how their lives
went wrong.

Me and the ghosts were making the most
of this rare communication.
I was teaching them ways
of the modern world,
they were telling of
lives led astray.

And I heard them sigh from a hollow tree
and I knew how lonely they were.
And I watched them drift
in the morning mist
as I touched upon
their despair.

And I sometimes find that I think they're there
and I sometimes find they're gone.
It's just the leaves
and the talking trees
and the river's secret song.

Brian Moses

HAVE YOU MET A WOLF?

A white wolf
at night wolf
beneath a moon
so bright wolf
did you have a fright wolf?

Have you met a wolf?

A grey wolf
a stray wolf
halfway through
the day wolf
did you run away wolf?

Have **you** *met a wolf?*

A brown wolf
a proud wolf
letting out
a growl wolf
did you hear it howwwl wolf?

Have you **met** *a wolf?*

A green wolf
a lean wolf
looking wild
and mean wolf
was it just a dream wolf?

Have you ever
maybe never
try remember . . .
have you met a **wolf?**

James Carter

SID

You've never met a cat
quite like Sid. He's a brute.
He's a bruiser. He's a bully, he is,
that cat from two doors down.

Sid Vicious I call him.
You should see the way
he terrifies and torments
our kittens. He's fearless.
He'd take the kill from an eagle,
the carrion from a crow.
If he was human, he'd be
forever behind bars.

When he walks, he doesn't slink
as much as plod and stomp.
He breathes heavy. He snarls. He scowls.

And don't you be fooled by
those delicate whiskers, those
pretty white mittens. Check out
those eyes. Deeper
than an old well. Greener
than a witch's brew.
And that coat, blacker
than the night when
the stars were stolen.

He'd pick on anyone, Sid,
anything, any size.

However tough your cat is,
don't let it out tonight.

Sid wins *every* fight.

James Carter

NIGHT SOUP
(A SIMPLE RECIPE)

Take . . .

A slither of moon
a nip in the air
a sprinkle of stars
a creak from a stair

Add plenty of dark
the slink of a cat
(with cold green eyes)
a loop from a bat

The patter of rain
the whine of a dog
the taste of a dream
the wisp of a fog

The whoosh of a train
a sniff or a snore
the swoop of an owl
then stop — no more

Then stir it around
and bring to the boil
season with cinnamon
add olive oil

Now let it go cold
and serve quite late
and all
      that is left
           to do
                is wait . . .

James Carter

ADVERTISEMENT FROM THE *GHOSTLY GAZETTE*

There's a special place where you can stay
when your haunting is over each night,
it's a spooky spooktacular guest house
where you'll sleep away the light.

In each room the curtains are shut
so the sun's rays never slip through.
We guarantee you a good day's sleep
with nothing disturbing you.

There's a hook on the back of your door
where if you've lost your head
your eyes can still watch over you
while your body rests in bed.

We have rooms with very tall ceilings
for ghosts who levitate
and to make you feel among friends
we can colour coordinate.

Grey ladies stay in one room
and green ladies in another.
Poltergeists are soundproofed
so they only disturb each other.

For those who like walking through walls
and would rather not use the door,
please feel free to enter this way
or even rise up through the floor.

We can cater for every need
and we're sure that you'll love it here.
Just don't forget to pay the bill
before you disappear!

Brian Moses

THE PHANTOM FIDDLER

(*A ghostly apparition said to haunt
Threshfield School in the Dales*)

There can't be an apparition
in our school.
We have rules to stop anyone
getting in.
We have keypads and an intercom
to keep children from harm.
Yet it seems that something
has invaded our building,
something that I heard last night
as I scooted down the street.
A screeching sound
like a fiddler playing,
laying down a curious tune
by the light of a magical moon.

And as I peered through the window,
into the gloom of 3B's room,
I caught a glimpse of children,
or were they imps,
dancing round to the sounds
a fiddler played.
And I had to admit
that the music captured me.
And I danced to the fiddler's tune
by the light of a magical moon.

Sensible people would have scuttled by,
they wouldn't have lingered like I did.
They wouldn't have looked in the fiddler's eye
or followed when he crooked his finger.
And I had no choice but to stay with him
as I danced to the tune he played
and the imps came too
as we danced in the street
by the light of a magical moon.

But something must have broken the spell,
something must have woken me up.
And I saw the imps for what they were,
nasty, ghastly, horrid things
that chased me all the way to the well
where I leaped in the Holy Water.

******

And that's where I was found
later that night,
when lights blazed over the hill,
shivering down in Lady's Well,
still hearing that phantom fiddler's tune
by the light of a magical moon.

Brian Moses

WORLD'S END*

Anyone living in World's End
must be used to impending doom.

No one makes plans for the future,
no one calls out, 'See you next week,'
because no one is certain
that they'll see next week.

No one buys lottery tickets,
no point if the world's ending soon.

I wouldn't want to live in World's End,
wouldn't want to be reminded each day
how fire and flame and tidal wave
could take my life away.

And everyone's wondering what it will be like,
the world when it ends.

Will skies crack open
and a fire burst through?
Will the oceans boil and bubble?
Will the pavements split and buckle?

I just don't want to risk World's End,
I'd rather stay safe where I am.

Brian Moses

* *There actually are villages called 'World's End' in Berkshire,*
Buckinghamshire and Hampshire.

ABANDONED THEME PARK AT MIDNIGHT

When you enter the roller-coaster ride
the seats are empty,
you travel alone,
as the cart hauls you up
to the top,
where you hang suspended
looking down at darkness
hiding the drop.

Till you realize, in the seat beside you
a creature has taken form,
something that looks like
the demon of death,
something that many centuries back
must have taken
its very last breath.

And you scream and scream
and scream again,
while the cart stays poised
on the edge,
and a voice in your ear
whispers 'Jump'
as the cart leaves you there
on the ledge.

Your lungs fit to burst
as the demon curses you
over and over again,
and you hear its voice
flowing through you then
like an endless river of pain.

'Feel it,' the demon shrieks,
'Feel the horror wash over you.'
And you know all at once
what the demon wants
is the only thing you can do.

And as you fall
the nightmare fades
and you wake to the morning light,
but each time you sleep
it's the same ordeal,
night after night after night.

Brian Moses

INTO THE LAIR OF BARON JUGULA

No light ever falls on the bushes and trees,
the flowers there are mostly diseased,
but I went there once for a dare.
I went into the lair of Baron Jugula,
past brambles that tore at my face,
past skulls, picked clean and grinning,
past savage hounds that bayed at my heels,
past the coils of a sleeping three-headed snake,
past monstrous eyes and fearsome fangs,
right up to the door of Baron Jugula's castle
where I stopped and knocked.

And the door swung open to reveal
the bloated, loathsome face
of Baron Jugula.
His breath stank and I shrank back
then remembered why I'd come:
'Can I have my ball back please?'

Brian Moses

THE HANGED MAN

I remember how Ben and I,
each summer morning, on our way to school,
would slip into the cool of
Gibbet's Wood, to find the hanged man's tree.
Nothing was certain, but it seemed to us
the likeliest place, and it felt so too,
always chilly, always dark and far enough from
    the road
to be silent.

We'd stand and listen, imagining we heard
a rough word or two from centuries back,
thinking we could see bleached bones or
a skull picked clean by crows.
All I know is that it stayed in my head at night
and helped give shape to the shadows
in my room. Ben said he couldn't sleep,
his dreams were filled with dread.

We'd try to forget, leave it alone, run to school,
but it drew us back like an itch that
we couldn't stop scratching.
I could tell it was some sort of spell
that was holding us there, maybe a message
we needed to hear, but nothing appeared,
nothing summoned us.

Years later I stood by the tree once more,
felt the same pull, as if there were a doorway
I ought to pass through, knowing if I did
I'd never return. I felt the hanged man's eyes
burning into my back as I fled. And I wish I'd
    known then
what I realize now, no good could ever come
from spying on the dead.

Brian Moses

A WITCH'S BREW

!! !! !! !! !! !! !! !! !!
!!   !!
!!   !!

It hubbles. It bubbles.
It boils at the double. Now all
she need do to make up her brew
is utter simplicity. Use electricity! Even
a witch will flick on a switch. No magic at
all. It's plugged in the wall. It's science,
you know. A cauldron? Too slow!
By name we should mention
her favourite invention –
in plastic or metal it
is a *KETTLE*!

!!!   !!!
!!!   !!!

James Carter

MY VAMPIRE GIRLFRIEND

With every breath
I'll love her to death,
my vampire girlfriend.

She's the girl of my dreams,
never quite what she seems,
my vampire girlfriend.

She's the girl I adore,
from her snarl to her ROAR,
my vampire girlfriend.

Though she treats me badly
I love her madly,
my vampire girlfriend.

And if she were the only
girl in the world,
my heart would be happy,
my head in a whirl.

My vampire girlfriend
is all that I need,
watches over me,
gets excited when I bleed . . .

We'll marry one day
and be happy to be
alive for each other,
eternally.

Brian Moses

CAN GHOSTS KISS?

If one ghost fancied another
what would they do?

You wouldn't get all those kissy-wissy,
lip-smacking, thwacking, sucking sounds
with ghosts, would you?

It would be more like watching
a silent film, although there might be
a hiss when their lips met.

And would they feel anything at all?
Would one ghost know when he'd kissed
another? Could ghosts recall
the sensation they'd felt
when they were alive?

And what if you were a ghost without a
head,
if you carried your head under your arm
and you fancied another ghost
with a head in a similar place?

Could two bodiless heads
still kiss?

Maybe the ghosts who were holding
their heads would tilt them sideways
like the living do.

And would they feel thrills
or just chills?

Would their lips be kissable,
the experience unmissable,

if one ghost fancied another?

Brian Moses

TOTALLY BATTY

He's a . . .

day-dreaming
night-scheming

blood-sipping
jaws-dripping

like-no-other
wings-a-flutter

soaring high
owns the sky

Will he bite?
Oh, you bet!

I'm Dracula –
and he's my pet!

James Carter

SPIDER, SPIDER

hear my rhyme!
Do you think you'll spare
the time to spin a little web tonight? From sticky silk in cold moon-
light? You weave away. You scuttle free.
Your artistry's an alchemy, of science, maths
and harmony. A masterpiece of symmetry. A
clever, clinging web design. A classic, Gothic
house divine! Your magic number? No sur-
prise — you have eight legs, you have eight
eyes. Little dancer, have you heard?
Your web's Eighth Wonder
of the World . . .

James Carter

MR P

Hey, Pumpkinhead,
    it's you again!
All starey eyes
and heart aflame.

And oh, that jagged,
    goofy grin!
What's the joke,
you spooky thing?

James Carter

SPOOK O'CLOCK!

When both the hands race round the clock
when shadows dance about the block
when you can't speak as you're in shock . . .
beware – it's *SPOOK O'CLOCK*!

When lunar's blue and way up high
when bats are buzzing round the sky
when vampires wake you'll soon know why
beware – it's *SPOOK O'CLOCK*!

When wolves are waiting in your dreams
when ghosts are dangling from the beams
oh, did I say it's . . . Halloween?
Be prepared,
for you'll be scared . . .
beware – it's *SPOOK O'CLOCK*!

James Carter

FROM THE CEMETERIES OF PARIS

Press herbs to your face,
bolt your windows tight,
hide beneath your bedclothes
if you should wake tonight.

For the night is bitter black,
the moon has fled the sky,
but darkness cannot cover
the horror passing by.

The creaking and the clattering
of carts on cobblestones,
the cracking of the skulls,
the rattling of bones.

Bodies thrown together,
no attempt to keep apart
nobility from peasant,
all are equal on the cart.

The wagons trundle slowly
to the tolling of a bell,
from the cemeteries of Paris
to the catacombs of Hell.

Brian Moses

NIGHT RHYTHMS

There's a rhythm
in the shadows
as they eat
away the light,
there's a rhythm
in the moment
when the day
gives in to night

There's a rhythm
in the river
running blindly
to the sea,
there's a rhythm
in the shutters
being battered
by the breeze

There's a rhythm
in the clatter
and the clanging
of the rain,
there's a rhythm
in the red fox
off to feed again

There's a rhythm
in your breathing,
there's a rhythm
all night through,
there's a rhythm
if you listen,
and it's inside you

James Carter

THE DARK

Why are we so afraid of the dark?
It doesn't bite and it doesn't bark
or chase old ladies round the park
or steal your sweeties for a lark

And though it might not let you see
it lets you have some privacy
and gives you time to go to sleep
provides a place to hide or weep

It cannot help but be around
when beastly things make beastly sounds
when back doors slam and windows creek
when cats have fights and voices shriek

The dark is cosy, still and calm
and never does you any harm
in the loft, below the sink
it's somewhere nice and quiet to think

Deep in cupboards, pockets too
it's always lurking out of view
why won't it come out till it's night?
Perhaps the dark's afraid of light

James Carter

THE ROOM AT THE TOP OF THE STAIRS

Dad promised us we'd have lots of fun,
long summer days of sand and sun
in our holiday cottage by the sea,
but there's something strange and it's
    frightening me.

I sleep alone in my room in the roof
and it's only a feeling, I haven't got proof,
but I'm sure something nasty has happened there,
in that silent room at the top of the stairs.

Mum says I read too many books
and no, she's busy, she won't go and look.
'Besides,' she says, 'boys are meant to be brave,
you'll frighten your sister if you don't behave.'

So I climb back up to my room again,
pause at the top of the stairs and then
hold my breath and push open the door,
then tiptoe warily over the floor.

I check very carefully under the bed
while an ever-mounting feeling of dread
leads me to turn the wardrobe key,
expecting some creature to leap out at me
and fasten its grip around my throat,
but a clatter of coat hangers, emptied of coats,
rattles its noisy chorus of doom.

And the room is cold, no hint of sun,
I wonder if other children have come
and felt the fear that I feel in this place,
like icy fingers brushing my face.

So I'm writing all of this down tonight
because something awful will happen to me,
something dreadful is waiting for me,
SOME TERRIBLE FIGURE WILL FALL UPON
   ME
the moment I turn out the light.

Brian Moses

A PLACE CALLED SLEEP

My mother used to say,
'Go to sleep,'
but where was this place called Sleep?
Quite often it was a place
I couldn't find,
even though I tried.
And often the harder I tried
the less easy it was to get there.

Was Sleep a city
that you were trying to reach,
or a lake you sank into
or a beach?
There was no road map
to consult, no signpost
pointing the way.

It was easy to get lost,
to take a wrong path,
and then when you found sleep
it was the wrong sort.
Something called Nightmare
would pull back the covers
and lead you into a bleak
and tortuous trip.

But there's no turning back
from a place called Sleep,
no escape (yawn!)
when it leads you into those
dark and dreadful dreamssssszzzzzzzzzz . . .

Brian Moses

AFRAID

Don't be afraid,
it's only your heart,
beating its rhythm
aloud in the dark.

Don't be afraid,
it's only your chest,
rising and falling
with whispery breath.

Don't be afraid
it's only your feet,
silently padding
the pathway to sleep.

James Carter

MY BED

I thought of reasons
in my head
why I shouldn't
go to bed . . .

The dark is way too dark.
My dreams are way too creepy.
My bed is way too cold.
I am in no way sleepy.

But now I'm here
I'm rather glad.
I've discovered
bed's not bad!

James Carter

HAUNTED HOUSE

Who it was, we never knew.
I heard footsteps, we all did too.
In the upstairs room, in the fading light,
something more at home with the night
crossed over that line between life and death,
making us tremble, holding our breath.
It happened the once, we never heard it again,
but once was enough, I was only ten
when I understood that nothing was certain,
a touch, a feeling, the flick of a curtain.

I looked over my shoulder for years, I still do;
there's a ghost of a chance that it might call
    on you.

Brian Moses

SCENES FROM A NIGHTMARE

The piano sounded a funeral tune, but nobody
    was playing it.

Footprints appeared in the dust on the steps.

A black blind snapped down and then swiftly
    rolled back up like a lizard's tongue.

Bulges appeared behind the curtains as if some-
    thing or someone was fighting to get through.

There were crackles and coughs from a
    loudspeaker high on a wall.

A single bulb from a chandelier flickered into
    life.

A fire extinguisher released a snake of foam that
    slithered towards me.

Words chattered from inside books and scissors
    cut the air.

I stood beneath a painting and felt something
    drip on my head.
I touched the spot – my fingers were red.

I felt warm breath on the back of my neck . . .

Brian Moses

LOATHSOME LULLABY

Come on now, my beastly thing
it's nearly time for bed
the dreaded day is on its way
so rest your ugly head

That blinding sun is rising now
and night is dying fast
so wave your silly little hand
at all those rusty stars

Have plenty nasty nightmares, you –
with creatures great and cruel
I love you more than dusty moon
my ghastly little ghoul!

James Carter

GOODNIGHT, GOOD NIGHT

Night, your things
aren't needed now
your limping fox
your blinking owl

your grinning witch
your dizzy bat
your moody moon
your alley cat

your forest full
of mischief magic
pop them back
into your attic

Off you go
without a sound
off to caverns
underground

Quickly, Night
be on your way
here's your noisy
sister . . . Day!

James Carter

MACMILLAN
Children's Books